S0-AHN-215

The Sleepover Club
Summer Secrets

Have you been invited to all these sleepovers?

Best Friends

TV Stars

Dance-off!

Hit the Beach!

Pet Detectives

Hey Baby!

Pony Passion

Trick or Treat

Be My Valentine

Star Girls

Party Time

Summer Secrets

Summer Secrets

Angie Bates

HarperCollins *Children's Books*

The Sleepover Club ® is a registered trademark
of HarperCollins*Publishers* Ltd

First published in Great Britain as *Sleepover Club On The Beach*
by HarperCollins *Children's Books* in 2001
This edition published by HarperCollins *Children's Books* in 2014
HarperCollins *Children's Books* is a division of HarperCollins*Publishers* Ltd,
77-85 Fulham Palace Road, Hammersmith, London W6 8JB

www.harpercollins.co.uk

1

Text copyright © Angie Bates 2001

Original series characters, plotlines and settings © Rose Impey 1997

The author asserts the moral right to be
identified as the author of this work.

ISBN-13 978-0-00-730993-1

Conditions of Sale
This book is sold subject to the condition that it shall not,
by way of trade or otherwise, be lent, re-sold, hired out
or otherwise circulated without the publisher's prior written consent
in any form of binding or cover other than that in which it is
published and without a similar condition including this
condition being imposed on the subsequent purchaser.

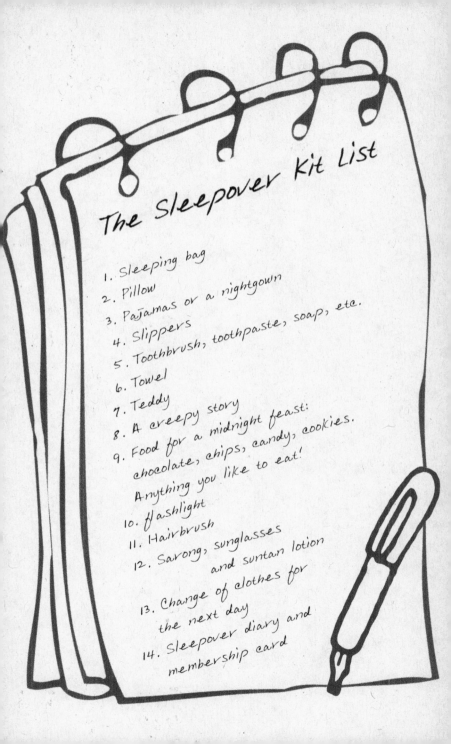

The Sleepover Kit List

1. Sleeping bag
2. Pillow
3. Pajamas or a nightgown
4. Slippers
5. Toothbrush, toothpaste, soap, etc.
6. Towel
7. Teddy
8. A creepy story
9. Food for a midnight feast:
   chocolate, chips, candy, cookies.
   Anything you like to eat!
10. Flashlight
11. Hairbrush
12. Sarong, sunglasses
    and suntan lotion
13. Change of clothes for
    the next day
14. Sleepover diary and
    membership card

1

Hey! Come in, don't be shy! I always love catching up with Sleepover fans. Oops, sorry, something's blocking my door! Let me shift this trash. You'll have to pick your way through the garbage bags. As you can see, I've been spring cleaning for hours.

You wouldn't BELIEVE what I found under my bed! Bald Bratz dolls with missing limbs, ancient board games, plus something very fuzzy on a plate, which I'm ashamed to say just *might* be a slice of old pizza…

Yeah, yeah, Lyndsey Collins cleans her room. It should be posted on the internet, ha, ha. So, what brought THIS on, you're wondering?

Well, I'll tell you, but I warn you—it's horribly humiliating. Yesterday all my friends came over in this big posse, looking incredibly serious.

Oh, hang on! Before I get into that, I'd better quickly remind you who everyone in the Sleepover Club is!

First comes Frankie Thomas. That's Frankie through and through, she just naturally jumps to ahead of me and you. (Hey, did you hear that? I'm a poet!) I'm not implying Frankie's pushy, but that girl could totally run her own talk show without any guests! She used to be a typical only child. But Frankie's really mellowed since her little sister was born. She's so-o gooey about baby Izzy, it's unbelievable!

Kenny's the youngest in her family. Her full name is Laura McKenzie, but to us she's just Kenny or Kenz. Kenny's a real laugh. She's also a soccer fanatic, a real sports nut, a bit of a brainbox, and as crazy as they come!

Next comes Fliss, or "Felicity", as absolutely NO one calls her! It's not like Fliss is a total bimbo, just a *deeply* dedicated fashionista. She's constantly worrying she's not pretty or skinny enough and going on stoopid diets, which can get just a bit boring. Fliss has the WORST luck with last names. She's Felicity Sidebotham, but when her mom marries her long-term boyfriend, a builder named Andy Proudlove, poor ol' Fliss will be Felicity Proudlove. Major improvement, not!!

Last, but definitely not least—tada! Yess! Take a bow, Rosie Cartwright!

Mom says Rosie's an "old head on young shoulders", which I think means she often acts too grown-up for her age. Rosie's dad walked out on them, unfortunately, so now Rosie just lives with her mom, her big sister Tiff and her brother Adam, who has cerebral palsy. When Rosie first joined the Sleepover Club, she was seriously down in the dumps. It took us ages to convince her we wanted to be her friends. But now she's really chilled, just one of the gang!

Phew! That's the intro out of the way. No, I *didn't* forget about me! I promise you, by the time I've finished telling you about our latest sleepover, you'll feel like you know me WAY too well!

Besides, I'm dying to get back to telling you what happened yesterday. Like I said, my friends all looked so serious that I went all wobbly inside.

"What's wrong?" I said nervously.

They must have appointed Frankie official spokesperson, because Kenny gave her a meaningful nudge.

"Lyndz, this is going to sound really horrible," Frankie gulped, "but there's no nice way to put this and *someone* has to tell you. The fact is, your room is a total pigsty!"

I was shocked. I don't tend to notice my room, to be honest. I just like, sleep in it.

"What's wrong with it?" I quavered.

"Well, this for a start." Frankie picked up one of my old sneakers and tipped it upside down. A handful of stale M&Ms fell out. My baby brother's always hiding stuff in our shoes. Mom swears Spike is half baby, half squirrel!

"Plus this!" Rosie pointed sternly at my wastepaper basket, merrily spilling trash everywhere.

"It's only old tissues and apple cores," I said defensively. "Not like, droppings from *plague* rats or anything."

Fliss crinkled her nose. "Lyndz, maybe you haven't noticed, but lately it's got really smelly in here too."

"I'll say," Kenny agreed. "If you're not careful, the Department of Health will stick plastic tape across your door and declare you a health hazard."

"Hey, stop right there!" I told them fiercely. I was really hurt. "I like my room just the way it is, thanks. It's cozy and homey."

Kenny shrugged. "Yeah, right. Homey. If you're a dust bunny!" She fished out several lumps of icky gray fluff from under my radiator and held them out with an accusing expression.

I was incredibly embarrassed, but I tried to put a brave face on. "That's just dust," I said breezily. "A bit of dust never hurt anybody."

"Dust breeds house mites," Fliss said in her prissiest voice. "And mites cause allergies. That's probably why you get those terrible hiccups all the time, Lyndz." And she started babbling about some special vacuum cleaner her mom got from a catalog, which sucks all this invisible dirt out of your mattress.

I doubled over with laughter. I mean, *invisible* dirt? Give me a break!

"Mom says you can tell a lot about a girl's personality from looking at her bedroom," Fliss went on.

She's not kidding! Fliss's bedroom is so pink and perfect, it's like being beamed to a Disney film!

"We honestly don't mean to upset you," Rosie said earnestly. "I mean, if we all help, we could get your room cleaned up in no time."

I'd gone into a major sulk. "I don't need any help, because I'm not doing it. I told you, I *like*

12

my room. So what if it's messy? I have more important things to think about, OK?"

But Fliss's remark stuck in my mind all day. She had a point. My friends' bedrooms do reflect their very different personalities.

Kenny's room is a total shrine to Leicester City football club, with eerie overtones of *Grey's Anatomy*. Can you believe she owns a life-sized skeleton? (Don't panic, it's plastic!) Kenny's excuse is that she's going to be a doctor like her dad, but the rest of us think she takes an unnatural interest in gross stuff.

Frankie's pad is TOTALLY futuristic. Not a pad so much as a *pod*—a silvery hi-tech space pod. If it was up to her, she'd probably come to school wearing jumpsuits with diagonal zips, like a girl in a sci-fi series.

Rosie used to hate *her* room. When her dad left, they'd only just moved in, so their house was still a real dump. Then one time when we were staying over, we all helped her decorate it. Now she says it's her favorite place in the entire universe.

Anyway, this morning, when I got up, I stood in the middle of my bedroom in my PJs and forced myself to take a good hard look.

Oh dear, I thought. This place is *seriously* disgusting. Three mugs of icky cold cocoa. Dirty clothes all mixed up with my dress up clothes. Crayons mashed into the carpet, along with a tube of body glitter. Plus, my pony pictures had been up so long, they'd all peeled away at the corners. And all my riding trophies were thick with grime. Yuck!

That's the problem with having four brothers. If you're not careful, you kind of adjust to living in a dump. My little brothers, Ben and Spike, are at the stage where they drop bits of cookie and apple everywhere. My big brothers are equally messy—they just drop *bigger* stuff. With Tom, it's stinky socks and crumpled-up artwork. In Stu's case, muddy boots and bits of tractor engine.

But today I've decided it's high time I set a good example. I mean, most of this stuff dates back to the last century! From now on I intend to be a genuine twenty-first-century girl. I'm going to save up and buy some of those really cool files to store things in. And I'm definitely asking Dad to make me a grown-up-type desk, to replace the old kiddies' one I inherited from Stu and Tom. Who knows—maybe my parents will even buy me that new computer I've been begging and pleading for (Yeah, well, I can dream!).

Anyway, I've made up my mind. With or without a computer, by the time I've finished, my new-look bedroom is going to make my Sleepover Club friends sick with envy!

But right now I need a rest. In fact, you must be a total mind-reader! I was just unpacking my backpack when you walked in, but now I have a better idea. I'll empty everything out, and you see if you can figure out what we did at our last sleepover.

Where did all this sand come from, hint, hint!

Ooh, and this teeny strand of pink seaweed!

Hmmn, what else is there? Old rubber flipflops, sunglasses, assorted pebbles and pretty shells …

Oh, and right down at the bottom, four absolutely ancient, hopelessly sandy adventure books.

Don't laugh! The characters might look like kids from a 1940s knitting pattern, but they provided crucial inspiration for our latest sleepover.

And let me tell you this sleepover had EVERYTHING. Sun, sand, sea and a crazy race against time to find hidden treasure.

Yeah, that's what I said. Hidden treasure!

No, I'm not joking. I'm dead serious.

Want me to tell you all about it? Look, shove those boxes out of the way and sit on my bed. Squish back against my pillows, go on, that's what I do.

Now are you sitting comfortably?

Then, I'll begin . . . .

2

It all started with a pain in my ear.

You know the kind of sickness where you feel very weak and everyone spoils you rotten? I *looove* those. Sometimes Dad buys me silly treats on the way home from work: candy necklaces, and temporary tattoos and sticker books.

Well, my ear infection was nothing *like* that. I felt totally awful, even after the antibiotics had kicked in. And I had to miss lots of school. I didn't mind missing classes, obviously, but

I hated not seeing my friends. Plus, being sick TOTALLY disrupted our Sleepover schedule.

I was praying I'd recover in time to go on our school trip. But when the day came, Mom said I was nowhere near well enough to go off to Skegness on a bus.

On the other hand, she saw absolutely NO reason to cancel the pool party she'd organized. She invited her best friends and all their little kids to our house. Which, if you include my little brothers, makes eight screaming, sticky-fingered kids under five in total! Lucky me, huh.

Things weren't too bad at the start. The sun shone, and the moms chattered and the little ones splashed around in our ancient kiddie pool, like cute little water babies. I just sprawled in a lounge chair, looking interestingly pale in my sunglasses, pretending to read a magazine. Also privately wondering how I'd *ever* squeezed into that teeny weeny plastic pool. If I jumped in now, I'd create a major tidal wave!

Then, suddenly the heavens opened and it

POURED. The moms scooped up toddlers and plates of sandwiches, and ran for shelter.

Unfortunately, Dad had started one of his famous DIY projects, putting our sitting room completely out of action. (My dad makes *Extreme Makeover: Home Edition* look like a bunch of wimpy amateurs!) So the pool party had to picnic in the kitchen.

Just imagine it. Eight screaming toddlers all spilling juice and trampling on sandwiches ,and occasionally on each other's fingers. *Total nightmare!*

I just couldn't take the mayhem. So I sneaked off to the bombsite formerly known as our living room to watch TV by myself.

But the TV was swathed in several sheets of industrial plastic.

My star sign is Libra, and I'm a really easy-going person. My friends will tell you that normally I take things like disappearing TVs completely in my stride.

But you have to remember that I was seriously

stressed out. My house was filled with rampaging rugrats and there was completely nowhere to run. And my ear still hurt, a LOT. And the no-TV-situation was just the last straw.

And I'm sorry, OK, but I completely lost it. Actually, I went totally ballistic. "ARGH!" I yelled. And again. "AAARGH!!!"

But no one heard me. This was because Mom and her friends had finally succeeded in persuading all the kids to sing Where is Thumbkin? at the tops of their cute little voices.

I started ripping at the plastic in a frenzy.

"I'm not asking for the moon," I stormed. "I want to veg out in front of the TV, that's all. But no! I have to unwrap the TV."

Finally, I'd peeled my way down to the last layer. Then, I dragged our TV to the nearest electrical socket and plugged it in. But all the channels had gotten completely jumbled!

Now I was *really* mad. I stomped back to the kitchen, glaring at everyone like the wicked witch. I usually love it when I hear preschoolers singing in their little off-key voices. But my heart had entirely turned to stone.

"Excuse ME for breaking up the party!" I yelled rudely. "But I'm still really sick, in case you've forgotten, Mom, and I *need* to watch TV, but Dad's sabotaged the channels!"

All the kids gaped at me in pure astonishment.

I could tell Mom was silently counting to ten. "Why don't you go and watch Stuart's?" she suggested at last.

"THAT heap of junk!" I snarled. "I'd get a bigger buzz watching Grandma's snowstorm paperweight!"

My brother's ancient Sony recently went on the blink, which means you have to watch programs through this permanent blizzard.

"I know," said Mom, in her best preschool teacher's voice. "Why don't you help yourself to one of those lovely juicy peaches, curl up in a comfy chair and read a library book?"

"Yeah, right," I sneered. "First find a chair, then—"

"I'm sure we can find you a chair," Mom interrupted, laughing.

"But I've read those books heaps of times," I moaned. "I can practically recite them from memory."

My little brother, Ben, slipped a sticky hand into mine. "Don't worry, I'll lend you my library books if you want," he whispered.

I'll just explain that Ben's favorite toddler fact-book explains *exactly* where your poop goes to, with very colorful diagrams.

"That's sweet, Ben," I shuddered. "But I just want to lose myself in a good story. You know, *escape*." My voice came out in a feeble little wail. To my horror I realized that I was going to cry.

"Tell you what," said my mom's friend Teresa. "I've got some kids' books in the car. I'm supposed to be taking them to the thrift store. My dad's been clearing out his attic."

"Oh," I said. "Erm…"

But before I could explain that this wasn't

exactly the reading I had in mind, Teresa had run out to her car. In no time, she was back with two bulging carrier bags.

Inside were the fogeyest, most depressing hardcover books I have EVER seen. No doubt they looked incredibly hip when they came out in the 1940s or whatever. But over the years, all the covers had faded to the color of booger slime (I'm sorry, but it's true!).

It didn't help that Mom and her friends were obviously expecting me to leap around with gratitude.

I pasted a fake smile on my face. "Oh wow," I said politely. "Thanks, Teresa."

And I lugged the awful things upstairs. I wasn't planning to read them. I just didn't want to hurt Teresa's feelings. But after ten minutes or so, I'd had as much as I could take of scowling up at my ceiling.

So very grudgingly I took a book from the pile. I guess it might be good for a laugh, I told myself.

After an hour or so, I heard a polite

cough. Mom was hovering in the doorway. "I reprogrammed the TV if you want to come back down," she said.

"Cool," I said vaguely. "Just got to finish this chapter."

I was still reading when my brother Tom called me for dinner!! I rushed downstairs, gulped a few mouthfuls of meatloaf, then bolted back to my room and carried on reading feverishly. The characters were trapped in abandoned mine, and frankly things weren't looking good.

When Mom suddenly appeared with the phone, I almost jumped out of my skin. I'd never even heard it ring! I glanced at my alarm clock and was astonished to see it was practically bedtime! How had *that* happened?

"It's Frankie!" said Mom.

I took the phone, still really out of it. "Hey, Spaceman!" I said groggily. "How was Skegness?"

"Oh, fab and groovy. NOT. Emily Berryman puked on the bus. All over my sneakers, would you believe." Frankie had obviously called to whine.

"Oh, poor old you," I said vaguely, looking longingly at my book.

Frankie sounded slightly huffy. "What are you up to, anyway?" she said. "You sound weird."

I explained sheepishly about my new addiction.

Frankie snorted. "Oh, those! Those books are so lame."

"Yeah," I agreed. "It's just that Dad—"

But Frankie started ranting. "Have you noticed how they all have samey titles? The Mystery of the blah, or The blah of Adventure, or The Secret blah? And it doesn't matter which one you read, they're all exactly the same."

"Yeah, but once you get into them, they're surprisingly—"

But Frankie wouldn't let me get a word in. "Have you noticed how the grown-ups in those books always find some convenient excuse to pack all the kids off to stay with this like, long-lost relative?" she said in a scornful voice. "I mean, how many long-lost family members have *you* come across recently, Lyndz?"

"Well, none really—" I began.

"Exactly!" said Frankie triumphantly. "And before you can say 'Bob's your uncle', the little kids are running around in their big baggy shorts and seriously sad sweaters, on the trail of some totally dumb mystery—smugglers, secret tunnels, messages in bottles, and I don't know what!"

Once Frankie gets on her high horse, it's pointless arguing. You just have to let her run down like an old-fashioned record.

"The thing that REALLY annoys me," she continued, "is how the girls always get so girly and upset. And the boy with the pet rat always finds disgusting old butterscotches in his pockets, and they're all fluffy and icky and I'm like—'DON'T put it in your mouth, Betty-Ann or whatever your silly name is. It's got rat germs!'"

I giggled. "He keeps the rat in his *other* pocket, you lamebrain!"

"But the dopey girl EATS it," Frankie went on. "Not only that, but she like, cheers up INSTANTLY!

I mean what is IN these candies, Lyndz? I think we deserve to be told!"

That *did* crack me up. In fact, I laughed so much, I started hiccuping. Ever had hiccups while you're still recovering from an ear infection?

It's AGONY.

"Sorry, hic (ow!) hic, Frankie," I whimpered. "Gotta, HIC (ow!) go!"

Whining with pain, I rushed to find Mom, who was helping Dad measure alcoves for shelves.

I hate being the middle child. My parents showed me absolutely NO sympathy.

"Oh, not again!" Dad groaned.

"Just hold your breath," Mom said impatiently.

Now I am the world expert on hiccups, OK? And I've tried every hiccup cure going and that holding-the-breath thing never worked for me ONCE. I was getting genuinely hysterical, but then my brother Tom came up with the most ingenious hiccup remedy since hiccups began.

He put one arm around me and drew one of his lightning-fast cartoons with his free hand.

And as I watched, hiccuping miserably, Tom's scribbles suddenly turned into a caricature of me hiccuping and going "Ouch!".

I giggled. "My nose isn't *that* big."

Then I clutched my chest. "Tom! You are *such* a cool brother! They're gone!"

"Tom Collins, Hiccup Wizard!" he joked. "That's me!"

"Yippee, yippee! I'm hiccup free!" I sang idiotically.

And I flew back upstairs to finish my book. Everything Frankie said was true, but I didn't care. I had totally fallen in love with those old stories. Actually, what I really wanted was to climb *inside* that world and stay there forever.

I was still reading when Mom came in to give me my last dose of medicine. She gave me a goodnight kiss, then switched off my light.

But I still couldn't sleep. I tossed and turned for a while, trying to find a cool patch of pillow. I wasn't depressed any more. The books had completely cured me. But I *was* unusually restless.

Which isn't exactly surprising. My head was filled with faithful dogs, and foreign-sounding villains, and flashing lights far out at sea!

Maybe I was still feverish, or maybe Teresa's dad's books had cast a strange spell on me. But suddenly I found myself talking in the dark.

"I wish all the Sleepover gang could have exciting adventures like the kids in those stories," I said. "Though in trendier clothes, obviously," I added hastily.

You know what they say. Be careful what you wish for. It might happen. And it did. It happened so fast that I was still tossing and turning when Mom got her mysterious late-night phone call from a long-lost relative ....

OK, I'll come clean. Uncle Phil isn't exactly a long-lost relative. But he's *terrible* at staying in touch! I think maybe he has phone phobia. He and Auntie Roz have been living in Australia and we hadn't heard from him for *years*.

But it turned out that recently, Auntie Roz had inherited some huge old house in Suffolk by the sea.

Mom told us about it next morning. "They're going to run the house as a B&B," she explained. "They've been working seven days a week since they got here, getting everything straight, and they've invited us for the weekend."

But Dad is a real home bird at heart, so he came up with all these excuses. He had exam papers to mark, plus his DIY was at a crucial stage, etcetera, etcetera. "You go," he offered suddenly. "And I'll look after the boys. How about that?"

Mom looked seriously tempted. Not only did she want to see her big brother, but I also got the sneaky feeling that she was ready for a break.

When we were alone (except for baby Spike, who doesn't count), Mom said hopefully, "Want to go to Suffolk this weekend, Lyndz? Bring a friend if you want. The ocean air would do you good."

My heart totally skipped a beat. That's what grown-ups always say at the beginning of those stories! That's how you know the adventure is starting! Was it possible my late-night wish could be coming true?

Don't be silly, Lyndz, I told myself. I shook my head wistfully. "Sorry, Mom. I can't just take one of my friends."

She sighed. "You're right. Oh, well."

I thought that was the end of it. But like Stu says, Mom's like our Jack Russell, Buster. Once he gets his teeth into something, he totally won't let go. And Mom was determined to see Uncle Phil.

That evening, she disappeared into her bedroom with the phone. She came out all smiles. "They said yes!" she announced. "Isn't that great?"

I stared at her. "Huh?"

"Your friends' parents. They said yes," she said impatiently.

"Erm, did I miss something?" I said.

'They agreed to me taking you all down to Suffolk, of course," she said, as if I was being particularly slow.

I was stunned. "You want to take the *entire* Sleepover Club away for the weekend? Does Uncle Phil know?"

"He can't wait. He says he and Roz really miss having kids around, now that theirs have left home."

"What about school?" I was shaky with

excitement. Suddenly my life seemed to be turning into a story. There had to be a hitch somewhere.

"No problem," Mom said absent-mindedly. "Friday's a teacher in-service day. I can't believe you forgot that! We'll have to get up early. It's a long drive to Suffolk. Where *did* I put that road map?"

My head was spinning. My friends and I were going to stay with my long-lost uncle in a rambling old house by the sea, and have a coo-ell adventure like the ones in Teresa's dad's books. And all thanks to my brilliant mom!

But before things could get sappy, the phone rang.

Fliss sounds just like a Munchkin when she gets excited. "Is your mom really taking us to the shore?" she squeaked. "That is so-o cool! I've got the cutest bikini! It's pink with little—"

I pretended to gasp. "Pink! Wow! You don't say?"

My friends were on the phone all evening, babbling happily about sunbathing and cotton candy and arcades. But instead of getting excited with them, I started to feel slightly fed up. It didn't seem to occur to my friends that I might have ideas of my own. I kept saying, "There's more to Suffolk than arcades, you know."

"Like what?" demanded Kenny.

Like, it's the perfect place for adventures!

But I just said carelessly, "Oh, Mom's got loads of local info. There's this old city that totally disappeared under the sea."

"Big hairy deal!" said Kenny scornfully. "I can't exactly see us playing pinball machines underwater!"

I thought my friends would fall over themselves at the prospect of a drowned city. Just like in the adventure books.

"Plus there's some cliffs that are like, haunted by ghostly sweethearts," I said eagerly. "And there's this church where that British Civil War guy Cromwell's soldiers totally blasted the door with their muskets. And once—"

Kenny made loud yawning sounds. "Bo-oring."

I sighed. Maybe when we actually crossed over

the border into Suffolk, my friends would change their minds.

I know, I thought. I'll get Mom to pack us a picnic exactly like the ones they have in those books.

I grabbed some scrap paper, thought for a minute, and started scribbling a list: *canned tuna, ginger ale, Spam …*

Three days later we were bowling down wide country roads with our sunroof open. It was very early still, about 8am, but it was really sunny and warm.

Suddenly Rosie said, "Aren't you hot in that sweater, Lyndz?"

"No," I said fiercely. Though actually, I was. Very.

"Those old-fashioned hair clips look cute though," she said quickly.

"Not so sure about the little ankle socks," said Kenny under her breath.

OK, maybe I'm a really sad person, but I felt like

I had to dress the part at least. I had to show a *bit* of faith. Otherwise how was our adventure ever going to happen?

It's not like I was getting much support.

Mom had totally put her foot down about the picnic. "I *refuse* to get up at the crack of dawn and pack a picnic," she'd said irritably. "Anyway I can't stand the smell of canned tuna! As for Spam, who *knows* what they put in that stuff! And you *hate* milk! No, Lyndz, we'll stop at a McDonalds instead."

So much for my excellent idea. Moms in books always get up to make their children's picnics. And OK, so I don't *generally* drink milk, it's true, but it sounds so lovely in the adventure books—all warm and frothy and fresh from the cow.

But I didn't mind SO much about the picnic. It was my friends who were really depressing me.

I did *try* to get them in an adventurous frame of mind.

"Uncle Phil's house is really near the beach,"

I babbled. "I wonder if we'll hear the waves swooshing at night. Hey! Maybe if we hunt around, we'll find the secret tunnels under the cliffs, where old-time smugglers stashed their loot."

But I might as well have been talking to myself, because my friends just gave me pitying looks, then went back to arguing about which to play first, One Direction or Justin Timberlake. Then Mom said crossly, "Hey! When do I get to listen to MY music?"

She meant it too! We actually had to let her play her cheesy oldies! I didn't know *where* to put myself.

But I haven't told you the worst thing yet.

Andy had given Fliss her very own cell phone.

Apparently, after she agreed to come on this trip, she went into a Fliss-style panic about being stranded miles from civilization. So Andy bought her a phone! A seriously expensive one with about a zillion different functions. So, of course, Fliss had to keep taking her new toy out of its trendy little case to see if anyone was texting her.

"Who'd send *you* messages at this time of day?" Frankie jeered.

"One of my friends, of course," Fliss said in a huffy voice.

"But we're here with you!" Kenny pointed out.

"I do have other friends," Fliss said snootily.

"Oooh!" we chorused.

Unfortunately, Fliss reread the instruction booklet and made the discovery that you could actually *change* the ring tones. Only, she couldn't decide if she wanted her pride and joy to warble Jingle Bells, play the opening bars of the theme tune to *Victorious*, or imitate a bird call. So, she asked an unhappy Mom to switch the CD off, while she experimented with all three tones again and again and ...

By the time Mom finally spotted a McDonalds, I was ready to throw Fliss and her precious phone out of the window.

Things improved slightly after we stuffed ourselves with burgers and fries. But the weather was really changing for the worse. We'd just gotten back into the car, when huge raindrops started landing on the windshield like tiny pawmarks.

"What if it rains the whole time we're there?" I whispered to Mom anxiously.

She laughed. "Relax! There'll still be tons to do. I showed you that booklet, remember?"

"My friends want to go to the arcade and stuff," I hissed. "They want to have FUN!"

But just at this moment my friends were having a major argument.

"Erm, Mrs. Collins," Frankie asked politely. "We are camping, aren't we?"

"I hope not," quavered Fliss.

"Absolutely not," said Mom firmly. "Actually, you'll be sleeping above the stables."

Fab! I thought.

But then Mom explained that the stables weren't actual working stables, but had been converted into rooms for people on vacation.

My heart sank. No picnic, no horses. This trip was a real let-down.

39

"Phil hopes you won't mind being in the annex," Mom said breezily. "They've got B&B guests staying in the main house."

Oh great, I thought. A bunch of boring bird watchers, that's ALL we need!

At last we turned off the busy highway.

Mom puffed out her cheeks with relief. "That's more like it. Now we're *really* in Suffolk!"

Despite the rain, the scenery was getting really pretty. All of the houses were painted soft pastel colors, sugar almond pink and primrose yellow, and there were weeping willows everywhere. Plus there was so much more sky than I was used to.

We were fed up with our CDs by this time, so Mom let Frankie play with the radio dial until she found a local station and we all sang along happily to One Direction.

But after an hour of twisty country roads, we were in a total car coma. It felt like we'd been stuck in the car our whole lives, lurching around hairpin bends and bumping over hump-backed bridges.

Finally, we reached somewhere called Pease

Magna, where we parked under a dripping tree. Mom wanted to buy some goodies from a village store, which had become a famous foodie haunt, apparently. My friends and I teetered along on our wobbly car legs, too, to buy supplies for our Sleepover feast.

On our way out of the shop, we read the ads in the window.

"Someone's selling a big flowery lady's dress," Kenny giggled. "You don't see too many big flowery ladies these days, do you?"

"Home wanted for adventurous kitten," I read aloud. "Tail and whiskers slightly singed."

"Oh the *poor* thing!" said Fliss in dismay.

It sounds really heartless, but the rest of us totally cracked up.

Mom came up behind us, clutching packages of squishy cheese and other weird grown-up snacks. "Come on. It's not far now."

"You've been saying that for *hours*," I moaned.

Ten minutes after we'd left Pease Magna, Mom turned down a wiggly narrow road, with grass growing down the middle.

Suddenly a pheasant literally fell out of a hedge in front of us. Mom braked just in time. Seconds later, a bunch of speckled pheasant babies fell out of the same hedge and went waddling across the lane after their dimwitted parent.

Kenny's eyes gleamed. "Pity. I hear pheasant is *really* tasty!"

"KENNY!" we all said at once.

Mom was still recovering when she had to back up to let a rusty old Ford go past. But instead of waving "Thanks", the driver just glared at us and shot past, splattering our car with mud.

In the adventure stories, country folk are pink-cheeked and friendly, and sell you fresh buttermilk and brown speckled eggs at the farm gate. Not the villains, obviously. They have scowling, unpleasant faces, and grating voices and greasy hair. Maybe the glaring Ford driver was our villain. *Eek*, I thought. If he was a villain, at some point we'd have to outwit him!

The narrow road became a dusty track, lined with ancient trees. They all leaned toward each other, forming a spooky green tunnel.

I noticed Fliss nervously clutching her cell phone. And all at once, I started feeling incredibly panicky and homesick.

We were in the middle of nowhere. There was absolutely nothing here except sky and trees. And rain and mud …

"Oops!" said Mom suddenly. "Almost missed it." She made a sharp turn, and suddenly we were rattling over a makeshift wooden bridge, between large weeping willows. A sign said "Willow Cottage".

And there in front of us, smothered with honeysuckle and climbing roses, was the oldest, nicest, most hodge podge house I had EVER seen.

I was terrified my friends were going to hate it.

Any minute now, they're going to moan about it being too far from the amusement park,

I thought anxiously.

But they didn't. They didn't say anything. It was like they were so stunned, they didn't know what *to* say.

Then Frankie took a deep breath. "Oh, Lyndz," she said softly. "It's perfect!"

4

Minutes later, we were looking over our new sleeping quarters, an airy upstairs room that used to be the old hayloft.

All my friends had the biggest grins on their faces.

"We can really stay here by ourselves?" Rosie breathed.

I knew what she was thinking. *Yippee! We can stay up all night and no one will ever know!*

My Auntie Roz beamed at us. "We thought you girls would appreciate some privacy. You've got your own bathroom downstairs, but if you need us during the night, just shout."

There was a scrabbling of claws on the wooden stairs, and a puppy appeared at the top.

"*Aaah*," said everyone.

"That's Gizmo," smiled my aunt. "We haven't had him long. He still follows me everywhere."

Don't ask me what breed Gizmo was. It was something Italian that I'd never heard of. I'll just describe him to you.

He was the color of vanilla ice cream with huge feet like fluffy mules, which he totally couldn't control. One of his soft, silky ears had accidentally turned inside out, giving him a puzzled expression.

He galloped up to me, all shy and wriggly, his tail wagging.

"That puppy doesn't walk, he shimmies!" exclaimed Frankie,

"Yeah, he should be a catwalk model," Rosie giggled.

"A dogwalk model, you mean," Kenny corrected her.

46

Fliss bent to stroke Gizmo, her fair hair swishing across her face.

Without thinking, I said, "If Fliss was a dog, that's the sort *she'd* be. A gorgeous designer dog with a sexy shimmy!"

Fliss turned bright pink. "That's such a sweet thing to say!"

Phew, I thought. It's not every girl who appreciates being compared to a puppy, even one as elegant as Gizmo!

"I'll leave you to it," said my aunt. "Come over when you're ready."

On her way downstairs, she remembered something. "You can walk to the beach from here," she called. "Just go through that old gate at the back and walk across the water meadows. Ten minutes' walk, max."

Rosie hugged herself. "I can't believe we can actually *walk* to the beach!" she gloated.

"It's not like, a boardwalk," I pointed out. "Just water and sand and stones."

"Who cares!" said Kenny to my surprise. "I just

want to see those waves."

We still had to decide who was sleeping where, so we tossed for it. I scored the one by the window, heh, heh, heh.

After we'd stashed our goodies out of sight, we all felt really hungry. So, we went through the connecting door into the main house, and immediately got hopelessly lost. There were all these funny little steps, and rooms confusingly leading into other rooms. Eventually, we just followed the smell of baking and ended up in this huge kitchen.

Mom and Uncle Phil were sitting at a big pine table, over cups of tea. Mom was showing him photographs of all my brothers.

"Next time, you must bring the whole family," he said firmly.

"Oh dear," Mom laughed. "*Must* I?"

It was weird. Their mannerisms were exactly the same. But my uncle was much older than Mom. Plus, he had one of those deep Australian suntans that look like they'll never wear off.

He suddenly noticed us hovering. "Come in! You must be Lyndz." He looked vaguely surprised. "My word! How these old fashions come back!"

I'd totally forgotten about my retro look!

"It's not exactly a *fashion*," I said awkwardly.

Mom tactfully changed the subject. "What do you girls want to do first?" she asked, as we nibbled on warm scones and strawberry jam.

"Explore this fantastic house," said Kenny immediately.

"If you don't mind," I said.

"No, it's perfect timing," said Auntie Roz. "The other guests won't get back till late, so you have the place to yourselves."

She started explaining about some big event at huge old house nearby, but I was too busy eyeing all the home made goodies to pay much attention!

There were blueberry muffins, chocolate brownies, plus a gigantic apple cake glistening with cinnamon and sugar.

But once my tummy was nicely stuffed, my thoughts returned to adventures. "Auntie Roz,"

I said shyly. "Do you have any secret passages in this house? Like one that leads to an old monastery or some smugglers' caves?"

My friends' mouths fell open.

"Secret passages, here?" Rosie looked around the room as if she was expecting a hidden panel to spring open there and then!

Frankie gave one of her superior sniggers. "Lyndz, honestly, you *are* funny!" So the others hastily sniggered too.

But my aunt took me perfectly seriously. "Hmmn, secret passages," she said. "Haven't come across any so far. But you never know."

"We have a ghost," my uncle said unexpectedly.

"Oh, HOW fascinating!" said Frankie at once.

Frankie goes a little over the top when she's with adults, like she's trying to be an honorary grown-up or something.

"Phil!" my aunt protested. "You'll scare them."

My uncle shrugged. "It's harmless, so they say. I haven't seen it myself, but people in the village say it has some secret sorrow that won't let it rest in peace."

I could see all this talk of ghosts was really freaking Fliss out.

So could my Auntie Roz. "Oh, don't listen to my old man," she laughed. "Let me give you a grand tour."

I want to live somewhere *exactly* like Willow Cottage when I grow up. It's gorgeous but totally homey. Plus, every window had a view to die for.

As we arrived back in the kitchen (by a completely different set of stairs), Uncle Phil said, "Did you tell them about the bikes, Roz?"

We perked up. "Bikes?"

He grinned. "Follow me."

Uncle Phil took us across the courtyard and unlocked a shed door. "Help yourselves," he said.

We found ourselves looking at a bunch of sturdy, old-fashioned bicycles, all polished, pumped up and ready to go. One even had a basket on the front! I was totally speechless.

Kenny was impressed too. "You mean we can

like, go out all by ourselves?"

Mom and Auntie Roz had joined us by this time.

"If you wear a helmet," said my aunt. "There's not much traffic around here, but it's better to be safe."

"Tell you what," said Mom. "You girls go for a ride and work up an appetite, and when you come back we'll get some fish and chips."

Fliss looked anxious. "That's a really nice idea Mrs. Collins, but we had burgers and fries at McDonalds. And we just had cake and scones. That's an awful *lot* of calories."

"Oh, a good bike ride will soon burn those off!" my aunt said cheerfully. "You'll be famished by the time you get back."

So we strapped on our helmets and wheeled the bikes over the bridge, ducking slightly to avoid traily weeping willow branches.

We hung over the bridge to look at the stream. It was flowing really fast. As we watched, a little black bird came swimming along with her tiny babies.

By this time I'd stopped being homesick. I was in heaven. I mean, Cuddington, where we live, is supposed to be a small town, but it's practically next door to Leicester. At night, you get that weird orange glow from thousands of street lights all like, bombarding the sky with their rays.

But this place was totally and utterly rural! You could just tell the kids from the adventure books would feel totally at home here.

We set off down the road on our clunky old bikes. I'll admit we were wobbly to start with, but for me, it was a genuine storybook moment. Though I *did* make a mental note to wear jeans, next time I rode a bike. Cycling in a skirt is super drafty.

The rain had stopped by this time, and the sun wasn't out exactly, but you could see that it was thinking about it. Now and then, little gleams of light shone up from the puddles.

"It's so *quiet* here," said Rosie.

"We'll take care of that," grinned Kenny, and she rang the little bell on her handlebars.

DINGALINGALING!

"Hey, there's a windmill!" Frankie yelled. "The sails are even going around, look!"

She braked violently, took a little disposable camera out of her pocket and snapped a photo. Then we all cycled on again.

"This is so awesome," said Kenny.

"Yeah," said Fliss. "But I hope we can go to the beach tomorrow. I really want to work on my suntan."

"There's no need to whine. My mom promised, didn't she?" I said.

"Oh sorree," said Fliss huffily.

I know I shouldn't have snapped like that, but Fliss's remark made me feel really crabby. I mean, we only had a weekend. We'd be lucky to fit in an adventure at ALL at this rate!

Kenny was ringing her bike bell, with that serious expression she gets sometimes. "Do you think they all sound the same?" she said.

We experimented. The bells were all slightly different.

"Coo-ell," Kenny grinned. "We can have a *wicked* bike-bell orchestra!"

And she started singing that really dumb song about a bell on a trolley, which my mom taught us when we were little.

We all joined in, jingling our bells loudly for the chorus. It was totally crazy!

Unfortunately, the scowling man in the Ford picked that exact moment to drive past, and we had to drag our bikes into the hedge.

"Did you see his face?" giggled Frankie, as he roared past.

"Did you see his sideburns, more like!" said Kenny. "Talk about stuck in a time-warp. Bet he was a big old tough guy back in the nineteen-fifties and he never got over it!"

"Tough guy?" said Rosie in amazement. "How were guys tough back in the old days?"

"They went around in gangs, picking fights and slashing seats in movie theatres," I said. "I have NO idea why."

"Stylish though," said Fliss wistfully. "tight

jeans, leather jackets."

I shuddered. "You think greasy hair is *stylish*?"

I still couldn't help thinking that the surly Ford driver would make the perfect villain. A poacher say, or a heartless kidnapper. But I didn't say so, in case Frankie did one of her superior sniggers.

We came to a steep slope and went freewheeling down, truly one of the world's *great* feelings!

"Yayy!" Kenny yelled. "Sleepover girls forever!"

But when we reached the bottom of the hill, I jammed on my brakes.

All I could say was "Oh, oh, oh!" I was totally tongue-tied.

"What's up?" said everyone.

"Ssh," I whispered. "You'll scare it!"

I put my bike in the hedge and tiptoed over to a gate at the end of the walk.

On the other side, grazing among the buttercups, was the cutest Arab pony I had ever seen. Everything about him was cute—his face, his dark liquid eyes, the way he moved. He still had the gangly legs and soft, faintly fuzzy coat of a foal.

My friends can be SO sensitive sometimes. I mean, they *like* horses, but they're not crazy about them like I am. But they waited with amazing patience while I tried to coax him over.

It was pretty obvious he hadn't been broken in, and he was really nervous and skittish. Yet, the instant I saw him, I felt the strangest bond.

This might sound weird, so please don't tell the others, but he was *exactly* like the horses I ride in my dreams. It was like I already knew how it would feel to ride him. And it was pure magic …

Suddenly, Rosie sneezed, and the pony gave this incredible buck, kicking up clods of dirt. He galloped away to the far side of his field, making scared harrumphing sounds.

I'll come back tomorrow, I promised him silently. I'll come by myself and we'll be able to talk.

"Erm, sorry to spoil things, Lyndz, but I'm getting hungry," said Rosie plaintively.

"Me too!" Fliss sounded amazed. "Actually, I'm *starving*," she giggled.

"Why don't we ask Mom if we can take our fish and chips down to the beach?" I suggested. "Like a picnic?"

"Excellent idea," said Kenny.

"Won't they get cold?" Rosie shuddered. "Cold fish and chips is icky."

"We can go on our bikes," I said eagerly. "We could put them in my bike basket and pedal like the wind!"

Did you figure out that I was being a girl in a book at that moment?

My friends gave me startled looks. But Kenny just said, "You're on. If it's ten minutes' walk, we should bike it in five easily."

We whizzed home at top speed, standing on our pedals.

When we got back, we quickly put on some warmer clothes. It was getting really chilly. Then Mom drove us to a tiny town. Just a street really, with a few dull-looking houses, a pub and a tiny and very shabby looking take-out restaurant. It didn't look incredibly impressive from the outside, to be honest. But Mom swore this place was famous locally for its fish and chips, so we all crowded in.

Ohhh! It smelled *wonderful*. I was seriously tempted to reach over the counter and grab a handful!

Luckily, Mom had no objection to us eating ours down on the beach.

"So long as I get to eat mine in comfort," she yawned. "It's been a long day, so be back by eight, OK?"

The second we got home, we rushed away on our bikes. I was carrying our fish-and-chip picnic in my bike basket. I made sure to buy a big bottle of ginger ale at the take-out. You can't have a real storybook picnic without gallons of ginger ale. It's like, a law!

It was hard work cycling through the marsh. Plus, the yummy vinegary smells coming from the basket were driving me insane.

We bumped and jolted through the weeds, past streams thick with flowering cattails.

Finally, we'd bumped all the way to a rickety wooden post. To be on the safe side, we hid our bikes behind some trees.

We all scrambled over the post and went racing breathlessly across the sand dunes, dodging between tall grasses and smooth driftwood.

"How come driftwood feels so soft?" I puzzled aloud.

But at that moment Fliss squeaked, "I can hear the ocean!"

"My lips taste salty," said Kenny, sounding surprised.

And at that moment we reached the top of the dunes. There it was—huge and glittering and completely awesome.

Maybe you get bored with the ocean if you see it every day. But if you live in the Midlands like we do, that first glimpse is a REALLY big deal. So, we got totally over-excited!

"YAYY! Sleepover girls on the beach!" Kenny yelled suddenly.

And we all joined in, shrieking, "Sleepover girls on the beach! Sleepover girls on the beach!"

Then Rosie got mixed up, yelling "Beachover girls on the sleep," and everyone collapsed into hysterics.

We stopped yelling as suddenly as we began, and just gazed around us happily. It was a very rocky beach, with patches of damp sand, and a thick scattering of seaweed—the lacy yellow and green kind, plus the luscious stuff that looks like a mermaid's hair!

The tide was out, exposing weedy rocks, and rock pools, and the shells of tiny crabs. Several white gulls were circling overhead, making their lonely cry.

"Our own private beach," said Fliss dreamily. "Just like movie stars."

Kenny went into her starving girl impersonation. "Food!" she said weakly, stretching out a shaking hand. *"Now!"*

"Hang on, Kenz," I teased her. "Food is coming!"

We hastily shared out the rations.

61

Frankie's vegetarian as you probably know, so she had veggie burgers with her chips. The rest of us had cod coated in crispy golden batter.

They give you tons of chips at that take-out place. Amazingly, they were still hot. A little too hot! We kept burning our mouths. But we were so hungry, we totally didn't care.

When she was finished, Rosie licked each of her fingers one by one. "We'll definitely put them in the Sleepover Food Guide," she mumbled.

A worried look appeared in Fliss's eyes. "I feel just a little too full," she said anxiously.

Frankie burped. "Me too. I drank that ginger ale too fast."

"Let's splash," I suggested. "That'll help it go down."

We weighted our trash with rocks, so it wouldn't blow away while we were gone. I don't remember the adventure kids ever bothering about trash, but then they didn't have to worry about the ozone layer either.

We didn't splash for very long. The sun was

starting to set and the water was FREEZING, plus the rocks totally kill your feet. So we went to explore the rocks instead. Mermaid hair seaweed makes great upholstery!

After a while, Rosie said reluctantly, "We should probably go back."

We started to climb back through the rocks.

"Sunset's so flattering, isn't it?" said Fliss. "You're all pink and glowing, Lyndz."

Frankie was looking thoughtful. "This is such a great place," she said. "Just a *teensy* bit too quiet. Do you think we can liven things up a little?"

"Like how?" said Kenny.

Frankie gave me a mischievous look. "An adventure maybe? What do you think, Lyndz?"

I wondered if she was kidding. You can never tell with Frankie.

"Erm, don't know really," I said cautiously.

Frankie sounded hurt. "Now don't pretend you wouldn't kill for an adventure, Lyndsey Collins. Why else did you bring those old adventure books on vacation?"

Yes, my friend was definitely trying to push my buttons. And I was just going to tell her to get off my case when Kenny broke into a huge smile.

"Oh, I read one this morning. Hope you don't mind, Lyndz," she added hastily. "I just *looove* those stories. They're so old fashioned, but you have to keep turning the pages."

"I *know*!" said Rosie. "You like, *hate* yourself, but you can't help it."

I was stunned. Well, how about that! I thought. My friends were secret adventure book fans all along!

And then it dawned on me. I mean, if Frankie despised those books as much as she said, how come she has all this expert knowledge?

She ADORES them, I realized suddenly. She's just worried about her street cred! This thought made me ridiculously happy!!

Frankie beamed at me. "So how about it, Lyndz?"

"What kind of adventure were you thinking of?" asked Rosie eagerly.

Frankie thought for a minute. "Erm, how

about one of the guests at the B&B turns out to be a dangerous international jewel thief?"

"No, I know," I said. "One of us sees a frightened face at the window. Some villains are holding a millionaire's daughter to ransom, but no one believes us."

"I'd like to find treasure," said Rosie wistfully. "Hidden treasure would be *really* cool."

Kenny put on her serious voice. "Not everyone knows this," she said. "But sunset is the best time to find treasure on the beach."

"How come?" said Frankie.

"Because you've got the sun behind you, so you can see all those emeralds and rubies sparkling like crazy."

Of course, we all started fanatically scanning the rocks. Everyone kept spotting gleams of color and swooping with shrieks of excitement. But when we examined our "treasure" close up, it always turned out to be pieces of stone or glass.

"That sunset theory is garbage," Rosie complained.

"Yeah, wet rocks *always* sparkle," I said. "Then you get back home and they're as dull as—as…"

"Things that are really dull," supplied Rosie helpfully.

Kenny scowled. "It's *not* garbage, and it's *not* a theory. It's a well-known—"

Her voice trailed off. She squatted down and started scrambling in the sand.

"Does this count?" Kenny's voice was sharp with excitement. She triumphantly held up a large green bottle with a cork in it. Rolled up inside it was a scroll of stiff, ancient-looking paper.

We'd found a message in a bottle.

5

Five minutes later, we were still struggling to get the cork out.

We tried using our teeth, our nails, also the awesome combined mind-power of the Sleepover Club. But the stupid thing *still* wouldn't budge.

"We'll have to borrow a corkscrew from your aunt," Kenny sighed.

"Yeah right," I snorted. "I can just see Mom's face."

"It's not like we're going to do anything bad with it," Frankie objected. "We just want to get the message out"

"*Exactly*," I told them. "I mean, suppose, just suppose, this message is like, a genuine clue to hidden treasure?"

My friends stared at me.

"Do you really think it might be?" Rosie breathed.

"I'm just saying *suppose*," I said. "But if grown-ups get wind of it, they'll totally take over. Before you know it, people will be scouring the beach with metal detectors. There'll be reporters, newspaper photographers."

"Cool," said Fliss. "We'll get our pictures in the papers."

"Don't be stupid. It'll be the total *opposite* of cool," I said irritably.

Frankie nodded. "Lyndz's right. We've got to keep this to ourselves."

"Think about it, Flissy," I said earnestly. "This way we get to have an adventure. A bona fide summer vacation adventure."

Fliss looked bewildered. "What do dogs have to do with it?"

"Bona fide means 'the real thing'," Kenny

explained. "It's Greek or Latin or whatever."

Rosie suddenly peered at her watch. "Yikes, we're going to get in so much trouble! We should have been back a while ago!"

We hurried back to our bikes and went rattling back over the marshes. The wild-flower scents seemed sweeter than ever in the dusk, and the sky was full of birds flying back to the bird sanctuary before it was totally dark.

We rode breathlessly into the courtyard. Mom came out looking stressed. "We were just coming looking for you," she said. "You should have been home half an hour ago."

"Sorry," I began.

"So you should be," Mom snapped. "Riding around in the dark in a strange place. Anything could have happened to you. Go and get into your pajamas. I'll come and check on you in a minute."

"Yes, Mrs. Collins," said my friends meekly. They started for the stables.

"I'll erm, just get a drink of water from the

kitchen," I said. (Well, the kitchen seemed like the obvious place to look for a corkscrew.)

But Mom firmly blocked my way. "If you're thirsty, use the tap in the stables. I've been driving all day and I want an early night, so scat."

I trudged over to the stables where my friends were waiting expectantly. "Sorry," I sighed. "Mom did her sheepdog routine and headed me off."

"We could always just smash it," suggested Rosie hopefully.

I shook my head. "This place is quieter than a graveyard. Make that *two* graveyards," I added gloomily. "If we start breaking glass, someone's bound to ask awkward questions."

Frankie sighed. "We'll have to wait till we're by ourselves."

"If we've got to wait, we could just buy a corkscrew in town," Rosie pointed out.

"Good thinking. We'll get one first thing," I said. "Now get your PJs on *fast*. Mom's coming."

We'd just dived under our covers when Mom came up the stairs, looking exhausted. "Everyone

OK?" she said wearily.

My friends gazed back at her with innocent eyes. "Yes, Mrs. Collins," they chanted.

"Good. Sorry if I was a bit snappy earlier," said Mom. "It's been a long day. Sleep tight." She started down the stairs.

"Oh, owing to popular request," she called back in a jokey voice, "we'll be leaving for the beach immediately after breakfast. So, I want that light off in five minutes, OK?"

We waited until we heard her footsteps fade away.

Then Kenny hissed, "I can't wait till morning, can you? Let's sneak into the house when everyone's asleep. How hard can it be to find a corkscrew?"

Fliss was horrified. "I'm not going sneaking around a haunted house in the dark. No WAY!"

"It's not haunted, you dumbbell," said Kenny scornfully. "Lyndz's uncle was just kidding around."

I shook my head. "I don't think he was." Don't tell my friends, but I wasn't too crazy about meeting a ghost with a grudge either!

71

"Kenz, I'm totally exhausted," said Frankie. "Can't we wait till tomorrow like we agreed?"

I sighed. Those kids from the books are always up for an adventure, no matter how tired they are. Plus, they would never let some depressed ghost get between them and a vital corkscrew.

But this was my world and the fact was, I was totally tired too.

"Should we have our feast tomorrow then?" said Rosie, who always likes to have everything planned out.

"Mmn, OK," we mumbled sleepily.

She reached out to turn the light off. "Night, everyone."

"Night."

SNAP! We were plunged into inky darkness.

"Eek!" squeaked Fliss. "I can't see!"

"There's no street lights, you nutcase," Frankie jeered. "What did you expect?"

"She didn't expect it to be so dark, obviously." I said. "Duh!"

"Yeah, no need to be so superior, Francesca

Thomas," snarled Fliss.

"Oh all of you just SHUT up!" said Rosie exasperatedly.

A huffy silence filled the room.

There were no curtains at the window, and I could see the moon floating in the darkness, looking unusually huge. After a while, I could see stars, too, looking loads brighter than they do at home.

As my eyes adjusted, I noticed a faint gleam on the dresser, where we left the bottle. The glass was catching the moonlight, which only made our exciting find look more mysterious than ever.

Where had it come from? I wondered. And who'd put the message inside? And *why*?

I mean, it had to be totally ancient. No one would put a message in a bottle these days. Not when they have cell phones and e-mail.

It's so unfair, I thought. The adventure kids have *weeks* to solve their mysteries. We only have till Sunday.

I punched my pillow. How could I sleep when

I didn't know if our message was an SOS from a kidnap victim, or a bloodstained map describing where to find hidden treasure?

But somehow, sleep crept up on me, because next time I opened my eyes it was dawn and I was listening to weird snuffling sounds.

All the tiny hairs on my arms stood up. Eek, I thought, it's the ghost!

The sound seemed to be coming from right outside our window.

"Hey, you guys, can you hear that?" I whispered to my friends. But they were still dead to the world.

I padded over to the window and almost giggled with relief. My "ghost" was actually a fox, sniffing around the trash cans! I think it sensed me watching, because it pricked up its ears, then went loping into the bushes.

I checked my watch. It was still early, but I knew I'd never get back to sleep. I don't know about you, but once this girl's awake, she's awake!

And suddenly, I knew what I was going to do. I didn't have to think about it. It was like I just *did* it.

I threw on my clothes and crept out into the pearly dawn. Ohh! It was pure magic out there. Everything still looked so *unused*. And birds sang their hearts out from every tree and bush.

I helped myself to one of the bikes, wheeled it carefully over the bridge, then rode like crazy down the road.

I was dizzy with excitement. I was cycling through the Suffolk countryside all by myself and I wasn't even scared!

Have you figured out where I was going? Boy, you know me way too well!

And when I got to the bottom of the hill, there he was, grazing among the buttercups, looking just as magical as I remembered.

A faint mist was rising from the grass, making my dream horse seem even more dreamlike than ever.

"Hello, beautiful," I whispered. "It's me, your biggest fan. It's Lyndsey."

The pony looked up briefly, then went on peacefully nibbling the grass.

I used my special horse-charming voice. "I *said*

I'd come back," I coaxed him. "Why don't you come over, hey? Come over and talk to me?"

I stood there forever, talking in the same soft, coaxing voice, and suddenly something wonderful happened.

The pony slowly started to make his way over to the gate, trying to make it look like it was just coincidence.

I kept talking softly. "Come on, beautiful. Come and talk to me. I won't hurt you, I promise."

The pony whiffled his sweet, velvety nose. I saw the tendons in his neck stand out. His super-sensitive nostrils flared, like he was receiving vital messages about me through the air.

I think his invisible advisers said I was OK, because the pony went on edging closer and closer, until he was standing so close to me, I hardly dared to breathe.

But, at the last minute, he danced sideways like a circus pony. Then, he stood hanging his head and harrumphing, like he'd totally embarrassed himself.

"Don't worry," I told him lovingly. "You can't help being scared. Look, I'll try to come back later. Maybe we can talk then."

I didn't have to turn around to know my dream pony was watching me as I wheeled my bike slowly up the hill. I could *feel* it on the back of my neck.

It hadn't worked out like I hoped, but I was still glad I'd cycled out to see him in the early morning dew. That is, I was sad, but kind of happy too, if that makes sense?

I burst into our bedroom, just as my friends were beginning to stir. "Come on, lazy bones!" I teased. "Some of us have been up for *hours*!"

"Cool! Did you nab us a can opener? Erm, corkscrew, I mean?" yawned Rosie.

Kenny was hunting around for her toothbrush. "Nah!" she grinned. "She's been to see her horse. Haven't you, Lyndz?"

I clutched my head. "Oh, NO!" I groaned. I had

completely forgotten about our adventure! How could something so important slip my mind?

Lyndsey Collins, I scolded myself. You are *such* an amateur, getting distracted like that.

"So we definitely have to buy one, then?" said Rosie.

"Mmn?" I was still miles away.

"I *said*, so we definitely have to buy one then?"

"One what?" I said blankly.

"A can opener—oh, *rats*! A corkscrew, I mean!" Rosie said crossly. "Lyndz, honestly! You've got a brain like a—oh, you know!"

Rosie's super out of it in the mornings. I started to grin. "Sorry, Rosie. We'll get one straight after breakfast."

"We don't have to eat breakfast with all those other guests, do we?" asked Fliss anxiously.

"I hope not," I muttered.

But when we went over for breakfast, my aunt told us that all the B&B guests had gone off to do this like, historic reconstruction at some local historical site. They just came back to sleep at night, apparently.

What a sad way to spend your weekend, I thought. Running around in silly costumes, pretending you live in olden times. Oh, well! It keeps them out of our hair!

"Hope you're hungry," my aunt said cheerfully, and she started putting all this food on the table.

I don't know about you, but in our house breakfast is not that big a deal. Well, let me tell you, this was an epic FEAST!

Waffles and maple syrup, sausages and eggs, fresh fruit and home-made yogurt. There was no end to it. And I'm embarrassed to say we wolfed it all down!

"Can't we at least help with the dishes?" Mom pleaded.

"Certainly not," beamed Auntie Roz. "Carrie will be here in a minute. She's a huge help, even if she *is* a bit of an eco-warrior." My aunt chuckled.

"Don't knock eco-warriors, they're cool," Kenny mumbled through a mouthful of crispy bacon.

"We know one personally," I explained. "Her name is Jewel."

And we told my uncle and aunt about how we met her at a protest to save this local beauty spot. Of course, then we had to explain all about the Sleepover Club.

Auntie Roz was really interested. "When my girls were your age, they loved having their friends over to sleep. And the things they got up to," she grinned.

"Don't encourage them," laughed Mom.

Unfortunately, by the time we'd finished our breakfast marathon, it was practically lunchtime, and Mom said we didn't have time to stop in the little town. "We should get started now while the sun's still shining," she said. "It's twenty miles to the beach at least."

"Don't worry," I whispered to the others. "There's sure to be a hardware store there. We can open the bottle when we get back."

"Aren't we taking it?" Fliss whispered back.

Kenny shook her head. "Lyndz's mom would be

bound to notice."

So, we all rushed to grab our beach gear. Soon, we were whizzing along sunny Suffolk roads with our sunglasses on and the wind in our hair.

Mom turned the car radio on just as the DJ was playing my favorite summer tune.

Ever have the feeling you're in a movie? Like, every silly little thing you do is on camera?

I felt that way for almost the whole weekend, like we were starring in our own Sleepover Club video. Everything was so perfect.

I know, I know. I was really supposed to be figuring out how to get a corkscrew, so I could solve a mystery. This was not consistent behavior.

But I'm a twenty-first-century girl, OK? And I wanted to have fun with my friends.

"I think you'll find this town has all the main Sleepover Club requirements!" Mom joked, as she drove around looking for a parking space.

She found one eventually, and we all headed

for the sea front.

Everything was bright and dazzling, like the whole place had been newly painted just for us. I could actually smell fresh paint, also warm, fresh doughnuts! Tiny colored flags riffled in the sea breeze and people whizzed by on rollerblades.

Fliss unexpectedly produced a bottle of bubbles from somewhere. She started to blow great shimmering streams of them, and all the little kids pointed as we passed. It was like the whole world was shouting VACATION!

We all had a long, cold drink in a café. Then we spent twenty minutes exploring the stores. Well, you have to check them out, don't you?

"OK, is everybody ready for the beach?" Mom said when we were bored with giggling over funny postcards.

"Er, yeah," I said. "But could we quickly stop at a hardware store? Kenny needs to buy something."

Kenny looked blank. "I do?"

"*You* know! That thing!"

Her eyes widened. "Oh, *that* thing!"

Mom looked annoyed. "Lyndz, I refuse to wander around a strange town, searching for a hardware store. There are perfectly good ones in Leicester."

"But it'll be too late by then—" I began.

My friends gave me warning looks.

"Sorry, forget it," I said hastily. "Let's hit the beach."

"Yayy!" said everyone.

Fliss sighed with relief. "I can *finally* work on my tan," she said.

We had the worst struggle putting up our beach umbrella. At one point, we had to chase it along the beach, like some crazy peppermint-striped wheel. And the whole time I was chasing it, I was secretly starring in my own Sleepover music video. I could actually hear the music playing in my head. I wasn't being vain, I swear. I was just really, really happy.

After we had the umbrella firmly planted in the sand, we did the whole beach thing. We dunked each other, screaming in the water.

We stretched out on our towels and basked in the sun like sleepy seals (we slapped on heaps of sunscreen, don't worry). We munched our way happily through the yummy picnic Auntie Roz had packed for us.

Then, all at once, it felt like the sun went in (which it actually hadn't), and the soundtrack in my head went totally off-key.

We are SO letting ourselves down, I thought. We have a mysterious bottle with a message in it. Probably our one and only chance at a real adventure, and we can't even find a simple corkscrew. I mean, how pathetic is *that*?

Mom closed her book and glanced at her watch. "Are you girls still up for the amusement park?" she said. "Phil and Roz are having a barbecue for us later, so if you want to go it's now or never."

And with one voice we yelled, "NOW!"

It's like no one thought twice. I know I didn't.

Well, what would *you* have done? Put yourself in our shoes. You've got two choices, right? On the one hand, you can have a great time with your friends, going on awesome rides, and laughing yourself silly in the fun house.

And on the other hand? What exactly? Oh, yeah! A stray bottle washed up by the beach, a bottle with a piece of paper in it.

An amusement park is like, a sure thing. But our message in the bottle was a totally unknown quantity. For all we knew, that piece of old paper could be blank. And, like Dad says, a bird in the hand is worth two in the whatever.

We scrambled out of our sandy swimsuits, doing all those embarrassing maneuvers with beach towels. And after we stowed our beach gear in the car, Mom took us to this really mega amusements place, where we had an amazing time.

We played the machines and blew tons of money. We yelled our heads off on the Ferris wheel. We shrieked on the swings until we were hoarse. And in the haunted house we screamed so loud, my eardrums will probably never recover. Finally, we went on a ride called the Corkscrew (yes, really!) and I was so terrified, I truly thought I'd DIE!!

We came reeling out through the gates of the amusement park, clutching cotton candy and feeling completely blissed out.

My friends were unusually quiet on the drive back. I was feeling just a little bit sick, personally. We were practically within spitting distance of Pease Magna, when Mom said, "Mind if we take a little detour?"

"What for?" I said in a grumpy voice.

"Roz says Blythburgh Church has a very special roof," Mom explained. She was using her patient preschool teacher's voice.

"Do we have to see it *now*?" I moaned.

"We don't mind, honestly," said Rosie hastily.

I felt a bit guilty. I mean, we'd been doing our thing practically all day. It was only fair that Mom should do hers.

The church at Blythburgh is almost surrounded by flat, green swamps. You can see its tower for miles.

"It's OK, you guys can stay in the car," I said nobly. "I'll go in with Mom."

Kenny frowned. "This is the church with the British Civil War bullet holes, right?"

"Yeah," I said.

"Then I'm coming, too," she grinned.

It turned out everyone wanted to see the bullet holes.

"Wow," Fliss breathed as we came up to the door.

It was pretty impressive. I don't think I've ever seen real live bullet holes before. And this huge church door was like, riddled with them.

"So what do you think?" said Mom, as we stood peering at these ancient battle scars.

Frankie instantly went into talk show mode. "It's SO hard to imagine all that senseless violence. I mean, when we're in the middle of this peaceful countryside, with bees buzzing, birds chirping, butterflies fluttering—"

"Yeah, yeah, we get the picture, Spaceman,"

muttered Kenny.

Inside, the church was really hushed and smelled very faintly of hymn books. We trailed around after Mom, not sure what we were supposed to be looking at.

Suddenly Mom hissed, "Look up!" And we did.

And the roof was filled with angels!

Not real ones, stoopid! Carved ones, made of painted wood. They weren't much like the modern idea of angels, admittedly. Their wings were up by their ears and they had these like, comical wooden perms!

Mom let us climb up some terrifyingly steep stone steps so that we could explore the priest's room. The stairs were so narrow, you banged your elbows on the walls. But, about halfway up, Kenny found a little peephole into the church.

"Hey, this is coo-ell! I can see your mom!" she giggled.

Of course we all had to take turns hanging out of it, waving wildly at my mom, until she hissed at us to come down again.

Then, she dragged us over to look at yet *another* door with scorch marks. Only, guess what! These weren't made by bullets. According to local legend, they were made by the Devil himself!

Apparently, one Sunday he'd tried to storm into the church in the middle of the service. But the churchgoers were praying so hard, he couldn't get past their holy force-field. So he was left outside, scraping at the door, and you can still see his huge fingerprints.

Yeah, right, as Kenny said!

But I'll admit those blackened fingerprint things were a bit spooky. And I think we managed to convince Mom that we were genuinely into it all, because she was humming as we drove back to my uncle and aunt's house. I think she felt really excited that she'd finally got us to do something educational!

As soon as we got back, we sped off to the stables to shower and change. But as we started up the stairs to our hayloft bedroom, Kenny groaned. "Oh, no! Corkscrew!"

Frankie whacked herself on the head. "Duh!"

"We are *such* idiots," I wailed.

"This adventure is totally doomed," said Rosie despairingly.

"It never even got off the *ground*," I pointed out.

"This is terrible. We're going home tomorrow," said Frankie.

"Thanks, Frankie, just what we needed," said Kenny in a sarcastic voice. "More pressure."

We went into a slump right there on the stairs.

Then Kenny said, "I've had enough of this. Let's smash the stupid thing now!"

Fliss looked puzzled. "I thought you said the noise—"

"No one will hear," said Kenny impatiently. "The grown-ups are over in the meadow, getting the barbecue going."

I felt a surge of excitement. "You're right! Let's do it!"

We all moved at exactly the same moment,

and ended up having a really undignified tussle on the stairs.

Frankie won (surprise, surprise!) and went charging up to the top. The rest of us were all still trying to get up the stairs at once.

"I DO hope it's a hidden treasure message, not a kidnap one!" Rosie was saying breathlessly.

"Yeah, a kidnap would be WAY too exciting," Fliss said solemnly.

"If it's a kidnap one, the victim probably kicked it yonks ago," said Kenny.

"Oh, yeah," said everyone.

"Erm, Lyndz! Where did we leave that bottle again?" Frankie yelled.

"On the dresser, you bozo!" I yelled back.

We finally managed to free ourselves and erupted into the hayloft, shrieking with laughter. Which is when we realized that Frankie was the only person who wasn't laughing.

"So come on, where is it?" demanded Kenny.

Frankie pointed silently at the dresser.

There was nothing there.

The bottle was gone!

6

The Sleepover Club has its share of ups and downs, as you know, but this was an all-time low.

I don't know about you, but bottles with mysterious messages in them don't tend to wash up at my feet on a regular basis.

We'd blown our golden opportunity, and we felt like total idiots.

But there's one great thing about my friends. They have this ability to totally bounce up again like, well, things that bounce back!

And that's exactly what happened.

"OK," said Kenny briskly. "Let's all go on a bottle hunt."

We stared at her.

"Well, we're acting like the stoopid thing just disappeared off the face of the earth, when it's probably just been put away somewhere."

Frankie's face lit up. "Oh, Kenny!" she breathed. "That's it!"

"Huh?" said everyone.

"Look around, you guys!" she said excitedly. "When we went out this morning, our room was a dump. Now it's all spick-and-span. Carrie, or whatever she's called, obviously came in to tidy up."

I was shocked. "You think Carrie *stole* it?"

"Duh," said Frankie. "Didn't you hear what your aunt said? 'Carrie's a huge help, even if she is a bit of an eco-warrior'; hint hint!"

"Yikes!" Fliss squeaked. "Carrie recycled our bottle!"

I covered my face. "Oh, this is so unfair! It's probably all mashed up by now. It's no use.

We're just not cut out for adventures. We should stick to watching TV and shopping!"

"Hey, I thought I was supposed to be the Sleepover Club drama queen," Frankie teased. "Isn't it possible that Carrie simply thought it was an empty bottle, and being a good little eco-warrior, possibly saved it for recycling later? In a recycling bin?"

Fliss went into peals of girly laughter. "You sound *just* like a detective!"

I felt a spark of hope. "Recycling bin? Here, at Willow Cottage?"

We stared at each other.

Then, we all made a mad dash to the main house, hurtling straight through the kitchen and out into the utility room.

There in a row were three big plastic bins, neatly labelled in black felt pen. One for wastepaper. One for veggie peelings. And one for glass.

I clasped my hands together. "Please, please, please," I whispered.

Kenny lifted the lid with a flourish. And right

on top was our precious bottle, sparkling in the afternoon sunlight, totally unharmed.

Everyone sighed with relief.

"Come here you little beauty. Mwah!" I gave the bottle a smacking kiss.

"Now nab a corkscrew, quick!" hissed Kenny.

We hunted around the kitchen.

"It's hanging on the thingy," said Rosie. "With all the kitchen doodahs, oh *you* know!"

She meant the utensils rack, believe it or not! We all fell over laughing. But, unfortunately, at that moment we heard footsteps.

Kenny hastily shoved the corkscrew into her jeans pocket, and I hid the bottle behind my back.

"*There* you are," said Mom. "I've been looking all over." Her eyes narrowed. "You haven't changed your clothes. What have you girls been doing all this time?"

"Erm," I said desperately. "Well, actually..."

To my amazement Frankie came to my rescue. "Oh, Mrs. Collins, it was awful," she babbled. "We thought we heard the ghost."

Suddenly, I was inspired. "Yeah, we heard funny snuffling noises. I heard them this morning, too. It *has* to be the ghost!"

Well, it wasn't a *total* lie!

"It scared me to death, Mrs. Collins," said Frankie earnestly. "I just don't feel comfortable taking my clothes off, knowing there's a ghost, you know, *peeking*."

I could see Kenny biting her lip, desperately trying not to laugh.

I have to say Mom didn't look too convinced. But, accidentally, Auntie Roz saved our bacon. My aunt came hurrying into the kitchen, looking for the salad servers or something. And galloping after her, with one ear stylishly inside out as usual, came Gizmo.

He immediately began snuffling around his water bowl.

"That's *it*!" Frankie shrieked. "That's the noise. Oh, I feel so-o embarrassed!"

"Yeah, whew," mumbled Kenny. "It was the puppy all the time."

"Well, now that the little mystery's cleared up, we'll go and get changed," I said brightly.

"Good idea," said Mom drily. She sounded deeply suspicious.

We just made it out of the kitchen before we collapsed in total hysterics.

"So, are we going to open it now?" asked Rosie eagerly.

"I think we should do it tonight at our Sleepover feast," I said.

"Yeah," said Frankie. "We'll do it in style."

"My deah," said Fliss in a posh voice. "We do *everything* in style!"

Uncle Phil had built a real barbecue pit in the meadow at the back of the house. He and my aunt were like, barbecue experts (I suppose they had barbecues all the time in Australia). But we still didn't get to eat anything for ages. I think that's an ancient barbecue law or something.

I looove barbecues. Grown-ups keep handing

you delicious savory goodies as soon as they come off the grill, still sizzling and smelling of charcoal, which somehow makes it even more exciting than food that has been cooked indoors. It's kind of like *outlaw* food!

Don't worry, there were plenty of delicious veggie options for Frankie.

But she spent most of the evening rushing around, taking pictures with her camera. And we all obliged by striking mad poses among the wildflowers. Gizmo's in most of them, because guess what! He'd recently started to follow *me* around, instead of Auntie Roz.

"You can be *my* faithful dog any time, Giz," I whispered to him, as I tickled his tummy.

The Sleepover Club is always up for a party as you know, and we all had a really enjoyable evening. But, I think we were all terribly conscious of trying to save ourselves for our grand Sleepover feast.

After all, this one was a biggie. We kept exchanging excited glances. And I knew what my friends were thinking, because I was thinking the same thing. We were finally going to open the bottle. Tonight we'd know for sure what was in that message!

But, it's surprisingly hard to leave a barbecue when the charcoal is still glowing. It's that Robin-Hood-camping-in-Sherwood-Forest thing. So, we lingered in the meadow, chatting, until it was almost dark. But then the midges started biting, and it grew seriously breezy, and suddenly Kenny faked this huge yawn.

"Wow!" she said, rubbing her eyes. "I'm SO sleepy. Must be all the fresh air."

This was our cue to yawn as well. "Me, too," I said. "Thanks for tonight, Uncle Phil and Auntie Roz. I had a great time."

We all gave Gizmo a last passionate hug, and Auntie Roz grabbed on to him to stop him from following us as we went racing through the twilight.

I grabbed a piece of honeysuckle as I flew past, and sniffed deeply. I think the smell of honeysuckle is the best, don't you?

We got ready for bed so fast, it was exactly like one of those funny old movies. All of us rushed around, tripping over each other and bumping heads, totally riled up!

Finally, Mom came up to say goodnight. "Any idea what you'd like to do on your last morning?" she asked. "I thought we could go to that museum at Dunwich."

"That kind of depends," I said vaguely.

"Oh," said Mom, sounding slightly miffed. "On what?"

Well, Mom, the fact is that by tomorrow, we just might be millionaires!

But I couldn't exactly say that, so I just said, "Let's see what the weather's like."

Mom switched off the light. "Sleep tight."

We waited until Mom was safely inside the main house. Then, we all switched on our flashlights, giggling with excitement.

"This is going to be the best sleepover feast ever," said Rosie happily.

"Come on guys," I said. "We're doing this right."

So we unwrapped all our sleepover goodies and piled them in the pretty blue bowl we borrowed from Auntie Roz when she wasn't looking.

Want to know what we got at the store in town?

Some of the goodies were slightly strange, actually!

We had pink and green wax bottles with super sweet liquid in them, a big bag of marshmallows that must have dated back to hippie days because they were in the *weirdest* colors, a bag of M&Ms, a box of little pies. (I bought those. I thought it was just the kind of thing that the storybook kids would eat.) Also a bag of plain potato chips, and a jumbo box of chocolates, because they were on special offer!

I placed the bottle ceremonially on the ground beside our feast. "Right," I said. "Who's doing the honors?"

"You are, girlfriend," grinned Frankie.

"No way!" I protested. "I never used a corkscrew in my life!"

"Now's your chance!" said Kenny, and she calmly passed it over.

I plunged the screwy part of the corkscrew into the cork.

"Yikes," I joked. "I feel like someone in the bomb disposal squad!"

I braced the bottle between my knees like I'd seen grown-ups do, and pulled hard. This is the tricky part of the operation. If you get it wrong, the cork ends up inside the bottle, forever.

But if you get it right—POP!!

"Yess!" cheered everyone.

I stared at the cork, totally astonished. "It came out!"

"Erm, the message," Frankie reminded me.

My friends crowded around, totally fizzing with excitement.

I felt like my hands had stage fright! I hooked a shaking finger into the neck of the bottle , and fished out the piece of paper.

It dawned on me that I must be the first person

to touch it for like, hundreds of years. Wow, I thought. This is so amazing! I cautiously unrolled the paper, and it made a dry crackling sound as if it was really old.

"Move your head, Kenny, I can't see," Rosie complained. "Is there a map on it, Lyndz?"

I felt a twinge of disappointment. "Uh-uh," I said. "Poetry."

Kenny was disgusted. "We went through all this hassle for *poetry*?"

"They often put treasure clues in poetry in olden days," Frankie said calmly. "Read it out, Lyndz."

I squinted at the strange loopy writing. "I'll try," I said doubtfully. "Erm, here goes." And this is what it said:

Look for angels above you
and devils behind
and the treasure
you're seeking
you'll certainly find.

"Well, that's as clear as mud," said Kenny crossly.

I was still peering at the message. "There's some little numbers and letters at the bottom."

Frankie sucked in her breath. "Of course!" she shrieked. "We are SO dense! Angels and devils. Duh!"

And PING! That little light bulb went on inside my head, and I got it, too. I started to grin. "Unbelievable! We were probably just inches away and didn't even know!"

Fliss and Kenny both looked at us like we were talking Martian.

But Rosie was bubbling with excitement. "Come on, guys," she coaxed. "*Angels above you*?"

"Oh, *those* angels," said Kenny, instantly cheering up. "Oh, wow!"

Fliss's eyes widened. "You think the treasure's in that church, don't you!"

We all nodded.

"Those numbers are probably like, measurements," said Frankie eagerly. "So we'll know how many paces to take. They always did that with hidden treasure."

"What do you think it actually *is*?" I said. "Gold and jewels, strings of valuable pearls and stuff?"

"Sometimes it's like, a stash of ancient gold coins," said Kenny.

"They dug up an ancient king round here once," I said. "Mom told me. He had his boat with him and all his valuables."

"Oh, I hope we don't find a dead king," Rosie shivered.

Fliss was looking doubtful. "This doesn't really make sense, you know," she said timidly. "I mean, why go to the trouble of hiding valuable treasure, then put a message in a bottle telling a complete stranger where to find it?"

Frankie shrugged. "So? Smugglers are always hiding their loot in those old stories."

I felt a shiver of excitement. "You think this note was written by smugglers?"

"Or bloodthirsty pirates, maybe?" said Kenny hopefully.

Frankie shook her head. "I don't think pirates could usually write. I think they just signed their name with like, a mark or something."

Rosie's eyes were shining. "Maybe someone stole it and then it started preying on their mind, but they couldn't own up because they knew they'd be put to a horrible death," she suggested.

"You mean he put the clue in the bottle to ease his conscience?" I said. I thought this was an excellent theory.

Actually, I started getting a little carried away. "He could have been like a lord's youngest son," I said. "But he had to steal to pay his gambling debts."

Fliss went all misty-eyed. "Oh, I bet he was really good looking," she sighed.

Kenny was shocked. "You're not supposed to *like* him, Fliss! He was a thief!"

"But Rosie said he was really sorry afterward," Fliss pointed out.

It was like she'd forgotten all her doubts. She was totally caught up in Rosie's make-believe! We all were.

Rosie nodded eagerly. "I bet he went to start a

new life in—in… I don't know…"

"Australia," suggested Fliss.

"Exactly. And as the boat sailed away, the lord's son threw the bottle over the side, saying 'I will never profit from my terrible crime, but one day…'"

Frankie elbowed Rosie out of the way and took over, giggling. 'But one day, five lucky girls will find this and become *humongously* rich!!'"

Suddenly, everyone went quiet. We stared at each other in the dim light.

"This is really happening, isn't it?" I said. "We are really, really having an adventure."

"Yes," beamed Frankie. "We really really are!"

"Just checking," I said happily.

"So now what?" said Fliss.

"We'll get Lyndz's mom to take us to the church first thing," said Frankie.

Something about this didn't feel right. The storybook kids would never just wait until someone's mom gave them a lift. They'd set out right away, cycling fearlessly along the dark, lonely roads. And if they got tired, the boys would break out the fluff-covered candies, to keep up their strength.

I sighed. It's practically impossible to have a bona fide adventure, when you're our age anyway.

But no one else seemed to think it was a problem.

"OK, so that's settled," grinned Frankie. "Now let's eat!"

I know, it doesn't seem possible, does it! Where DO we put it?

I have no idea, but we did. We *always* do!

We feasted happily on all the weird candies, weaving wild daydreams about the things we'd do when we became millionaires.

"I'll run my own riding stables," I said. "No question."

"Go to Hollywood and make films," Frankie mumbled through a mouthful of pie.

Fliss didn't have to think about it. "Start my own incredibly successful design label," she beamed.

"Me? Oh, I think I'd probably buy Leicester City football club," said Kenny, casually.

I noticed Rosie smiling to herself. "I'd buy my

109

brother the very latest state-of-the-art computer," she said. "So he can be really independent."

See what I mean about Rosie? She just can't help being grown-up, even in her daydreams.

But it wasn't long before we were all yawning. For real this time.

"Sorry to be a party pooper," said Kenny. "But I've got to crash. I'm exhausted."

We switched off our flashlights, and settled down to go to sleep.

Lying in the dark often makes Frankie really chatty. (NO!!) Her voice floated through the dark. "When you think about it," she said drowsily, "we're exactly like the kids in the books. I mean, they're always stuffing their faces and so are we."

"Mmn," we all said sleepily.

"And our characters are so similar, it's spooky!" she continued. "Fliss is the girly one, and Kenny is like a total tomboy, and Lyndz is animal crazy, and Rosie's like the motherly sensible one."

I heard Kenny snort. "Yeah, so which one are you, then?"

Frankie sounded smug. "I'm the brainy one who unravels the clues, of course!"

So we all threw our pillows at her. Then, of course, we had to get up and find them again!

But, as I drifted off to sleep, my mind was buzzing with questions.

In that book world, anything is possible. Ten-year-old kids go camping by themselves and no one seems to notice. They even capture grown-up criminals, and march them off to the police.

But this was our world, the real world.

Did we really think we could walk into a church and help ourselves to valuable treasure, just because we found a clue in a bottle?

Could it really be that easy? The others seemed to think so, and I wanted to believe them.

But suddenly, as I lay there in the dark, I wasn't so sure.

7

Early the next morning we rushed to find Mom, and begged her to take us to Blythburgh Church.

"What brought this on?" she said suspiciously.

Frankie clasped her hands. "It was just such a great experience, Mrs. Collins," she said. "We just *have* to see that roof once more before we go home."

"I mean, who knows when we'll come back?" Kenny said in a tragic voice.

Auntie Roz laughed. "I'll take them! You stay

here," she said to Mom. "Pour yourself another cup of coffee and chat with Phil."

She picked up her car keys, and we all set off to Blythburgh in my uncle and aunt's beat-up old van. "It's Sunday, so we'll have to nip in between services," she explained over the roar of the engine. She gave us a comical look. "Unless you actually wanted to go to church?"

We hastily shook our heads.

Auntie Roz grinned. "So, now that we're alone, do you think you could spill the beans? You five girls are fizzing like Roman candles, and the suspense is killing me!"

I don't know why we decided to take Auntie Roz into our confidence. but we told her everything.

She was fascinated to hear about the bottle. "I did wonder where my corkscrew had gone," she said humorously. She was genuinely astonished when we read her the message, but she didn't seem too confident that we'd find hidden treasure at Blythburgh Church.

"Still, there's no harm in looking," she said

cheerfully. "And on the way back I'll buy you some ice cream, how about that!"

She's worried we'll be disappointed, I thought. I got this horrible sinking feeling. How could I have been so stupid as to think we'd find treasure in a church?

In our hayloft, alone in the night, I let my imagination carry me over the rainbow. But now it was morning in the real world, and we were driving along a busy main road, and I just knew it was never going to happen.

From their subdued expressions, I got the impression my friends were feeling the same way.

At last, the van crunched over the gravel into the church parking lot. Churchgoers were already streaming out.

We jumped out and followed Auntie Roz through the crowd. I was feeling totally desperate by this time. "Look, let's forget about it," I hissed to the others. "It was a stupid idea."

"Look, we're here, aren't we?" said Frankie angrily. "And I'm not a quitter, even if you are."

Rosie sounded reproachful. "We can at least look, since we're here, Lyndz."

And my friends went wandering off with Auntie Roz.

I stayed glued by the door, feeling like I had "I'm stupid" written all over me.

Little choirboys were practicing a hymn at the far end of the church. And I could see the priest talking earnestly to two old ladies.

I started feeling uncomfortable about taking up his valuable church space when I didn't attend this actual church, so I drifted off to the side and pretended to look at some postcards they had for sale.

Wonder if they have a postcard of the angels, I thought. I could get one for Dad.

I started to search along the rack, and suddenly this card fell at my feet.

It wasn't a picture postcard. It just had writing on it. My heartbeat went into overdrive. I fumbled frantically in my bag until I found the message. The writing on the card was exactly the same!

Only this message was strictly twenty-first century.

And underneath was the number of the local radio station.

There was also a lot of info about the Tourist Board, and all the exciting places you could visit in Suffolk that I didn't even try to take in.

I rushed to find the others. "Our treasure's for real!" I squeaked. "I mean, it's actually a publicity stunt for the Tourist Board. But we won a prize!"

I dragged them outside. "See these!" I pointed to the numbers at the bottom of the original message. "They're not measurements at all. It's the wavelength of the radio station we were listening to on the way down! Isn't that *amazing*!" I was practically jumping up and down.

The others still looked a bit dazed.

"It's fantastic," said my aunt warmly. "Not quite what you girls were expecting, I know. You must call the station as soon as we get back to the house."

Fliss started to grin. "We can do better than that!"

And as if she'd owned a cell phone her whole life, she fished it out of her jeans pocket, turned it on, and carefully punched in the number.

"Oh, good morning," she said politely. "We're currently visiting the Suffolk area, and we're calling to claim our prize. No, I don't mind holding…"

Isn't it incredible?!

We'd been having a totally modern adventure all along!

OK, so our treasure wasn't quite as romantic as we hoped. But if you think about it, it's way more useful. At least we got to *keep* this prize. I don't REALLY think we'd have been allowed to keep actual gold and rubies, do you? Not in this world!

Only, you're going to have to wait a little longer before I give you the juicy details of the humongously generous prize we received from the Suffolk Tourist Board, because I've got

some eensy weensy loose ends to tie up first.
But you guessed that already, didn't you!

8

"Do you want the bikes, girls, or should I lock them up?" Uncle Phil asked us after lunch.

Mom looked doubtful. "We'll have to leave soon."

My friends were all sprawled on a big sofa playing with Gizmo.

"I'm too stuffed to move," Kenny groaned.

This was the opportunity I'd been waiting for.

"Mo-om," I said pleadingly. "Is there time for me to have a very quick ride? I won't be more than ten minutes, honestly."

(Well, I couldn't possibly go without saying goodbye to my dream horse now, could I?)

"All right, but not a minute longer," said Mom. "You all have school tomorrow."

"I'll ride like the wind!" I said eagerly, then I blushed. I'd accidentally slipped into book-speak without thinking.

"I'll go with her, don't worry," said Uncle Phil. "Want to go anywhere in particular, Lyndz?" he grinned.

We went racing off down the road, me and my Australian uncle. Me first, him following. Both of us talking a mile a minute. I'd gotten over my annoyance at having company. Actually, it was great to have a chance to chat.

I was telling him what a great time I'd had.

Uncle Phil said, "You must get your mom to bring you again." He meant it too. And, with a rush of happiness, it dawned on me that I had just acquired a really cool uncle.

Which is probably why I didn't see the grumpy Ford driver glaring by the gate until it was too late.

"What do you think you're up to, girl?" he demanded.

To my amazement he gave my uncle a friendly grin. "Arternoon, Phil," he said. "This that little niece you were talking about?"

"Yes, this is Lyndsey," said my uncle.

"I suppose she's come to see Eeyore here." The old man gave me a searching look. "Pretty little old boy, ain't he?"

"He's beautiful," I said with feeling. But I couldn't help saying, "Why the heck did you call him Eeyore?"

Because, if that pony was mine, I'd have named him something really nice. I wouldn't have called him after some gloomy donkey.

The old man laughed, a rusty laugh, as if he didn't get much practice. "Oh Lord, he weren't mine to name, dear. He belongs to my granddaughter, Amy. She's been in the hospital these last three months. We've all been worried about her. I promised I'd take care of Eeyore for her while she was sick, but today we just had some good news, and she's a-coming out next Friday."

"Ohh," I said. "So that's why you—"

Then I went bright red. I was going to say, "So THAT'S why you were looking so bad-tempered."

Instead I said hastily, "So that's why you're up and down the road all the time."

"You like horses, then, do you, Lyndsey?" he asked.

"I *love* them," I said. "I go riding every chance I get."

"You want to come back in a few months," he suggested to my surprise. "We're a-going to break that little pony in, when Amy gets her strength back. You and she can maybe get together."

While we were chatting by the gate, the sweetest thing happened. Like all horses, the dream horse was really nosy. He came sidling up, to see what was going on, whiffling his super-sensitive nostrils.

"Let him smell your hand," said the old man. "Go on, let him know you're his friend."

Very slowly, I reached out my hand, and to my

delight Eeyore actually brushed it with his velvety nose, then danced away on his gangly foal legs.

I touched my hand to my cheek. I couldn't stop smiling.

"We'd better go," said Uncle Phil. "Your mom's waiting."

I started pushing my bike up the hill. "Erm, I'm really glad Amy's getting better," I called. "I'd like to meet her when I come again."

The old man gave me a brief wave. He still looked like a big, elderly teddy-boy, but he didn't look nearly so villainous somehow.

That's a major difference between our world and the book world, where villains are instantly recognizable because of their rat-like features. In our world, you probably pass villains in the street all the time and never know it.

When we reached Willow Cottage, Uncle Phil said to run and tell Mom that I was back, while he put the bikes away.

But when I walked in through the front door, there was nobody there. I wandered in and out of the rooms calling, but no one answered.

I started to get slightly spooked. It was like they'd all vanished off the face of the earth.

I just decided to go across to the stables to see if they were there, when I heard the tiniest movement behind me.

I spun around—and found myself two metres away from the ghost.

OK, as ghosts go it wasn't incredibly old fashioned, but a ghost is a ghost, right? And the fact that this ghost was a freckle-faced boy, about my own age, wearing baggy 1940s shorts and a tragic beige sweater, didn't make it any less terrifying.

It made it worse, actually. It was like I was being haunted by a character from the adventure books!

I just stood there, gaping at him, almost fainting with fright. Suddenly he put his hand into his pocket. For a moment, I thought he was going to hand me a candy, or perhaps (eek!) let me hold his pet rat. Instead, he pulled out a large home-made catapult.

"Don't shoot!" I squeaked ridiculously.

"Oh, ha, ha, great joke," he snorted. "My parents won't even let me fire it at a tin can." He scowled. "That's just SO typical. They drag me into the middle of nowhere to take part in some stupid historical reconstruction, and make me wear these stupid prickly clothes, and they STILL never let me have any fun!"

And the boy stomped out into the garden, muttering angrily.

Suddenly, I started to laugh. I couldn't help it.

"That was SO weird," I giggled to myself.

Wait till I told my friends! And I went racing off to find them, grinning from ear to ear.

I told you those old adventure books were crucial, didn't I? But before you go, I've got a confession to make.

Remember I said I wished my parents would get me a computer? Well, I was stringing you along a teensy bit.

You see, I knew all along they could never afford to buy one in a million years. But now it completely doesn't matter. Why? Because under this piece of plastic sheeting—tada!

Hidden treasure!

Now tell me *honestly*, have you *ever* seen such a cool computer in your life?

There were other prizes on offer, depending on which bottle you found: a balloon trip over the Suffolk countryside, a meal in a swanky Aldeburgh restaurant. But somehow, our luck was in, and we got *this* totally awesome machine.

The great thing is, all my friends have computers already, so they were really chilled about me keeping it here. It was even their idea.

And yes, maybe it did have something to do with me cleaning up my room. It's a coo-ell twenty-first-century machine, and like I said at the start, I've made up my mind to be a genuine twenty-first-century girl (who also happens to looove old-fashioned adventure stories!).

Oh well, better get back to filling these trash

bags. Take care, won't you? It's been great talking to you.

Bye—and have a really great summer, yeah?!!

Roll the windows down, get your shades on. Fliss's top tunes for a summer-vacation drive!

'Mercy'...Duffy

'Suddenly I see'...KT Tunstall

'Smile'...Lilly Allen

'Honey Honey'..Amanda Seyfried

'Mama Mia'..Abba

And something to keep the oldies happy. Get retro with these top tunes!

'Club Tropicana'...Wham!

'Walking on Sunshine'...........................Katrina and the Waves

'Rio'..Duran Duran

'Summer Holiday'......................Cliff Richard and the Shadows

'Califonia Girls'...The Beach Boys

Fliss XO

Chill out in the sun with Frankie's cool strawberry mousse

You will need:

- ¼ litre (1/2 pint) heavy cream
- 8oz (220g) strawberries (hulled)
- 3 tablespoons powdered sugar

Here's what you do:

1. Whisk the cream until it's thick and stands up in peaks.
2. Put the hulled strawberries in a food processor and pulp until smooth.
3. Add the strawberries to the whipped cream, and stir in the powdered sugar.
4. Spoon the mixture into glasses, and put in the fridge for two hours.
5. Eat!

Frankie xo

Up for an armchair adventure? Get nostalgic with Lyndz's top reads

The Lion, the Witch and the Wardrobe	C S Lewis
The Castle of Adventure	Enid Blyton
Swallows and Amazons	Arthur Ransome
Five Go to Smuggler's Top	Enid Blyton
The Secret Garden	Frances Hodgson Burnett
The Wolves of Willoughby Chase	Joan Aiken
Look Out, Secret Seven	Enid Blyton

Lyndz xo

Rosie's treasure hunt game

Here's what you do:

1. Get into two groups
2. One group hides some 'treasure'* and makes a list of clues.**
3. The second group has to follow the clues to the treasure.
4. Swap, so the treasure seekers now lay a trail for the other team
5. Time each team—see who gets to the treasure the fastest.

*This could be a favorite object or a bag of candy to share

**Draw a map, make up some written clues, or lay a trail using stones and leaves

Don't let rain get in the way! You can hunt for treasure round your house too.

Rosie xo

Want to write your own secret message? Check out Kenny's invisible ink!

1 Squeeze the juice of one or two lemons onto a small plate.

2 Get a small paintbrush and, using the lemon juice, write a message on a white piece of paper.

3 To read the message, hold the paper into the sunlight – the words written in lemon juice will soon appear!

Kenny

xo

Join The SleePover Club